Too Much Tubular!

BRAVE BOOKS

DOM-A-TRON

THE OLD ISLANDS

Burrycanter

Doomsdome

UTOPIA

Freedom Island

WIGGAMORE WOOD

SUMA SAVANNA

Rushington

Furenzy Park

Hive Hav

Toke-A-Toke

WonderWell

Capitol

Deserted Desert

RAKA RAIN FOREST

Mushroom Village

Mt. Avalerif

Sky Tree

Snapfast Meadow

Starlotte City

CAR-A-LAGO COAST

Gray Landing

Home of the Brave

Welcome to Freedom Island, Home of the Brave, where good battles evil and truth prevails. Join Team BRAVE as they travel to Furenzy Park to solve the Tubular problem. Complete the BRAVE Challenge at the end of the book to learn more!

Watch this video for an introduction to the story and BRAVE Universe!

Saga Three: Tubular
Book 10

Too Much Tubular!

On the map: Shivermore, Nogard Cavern, MONOCK MOUNTAINS, Meltonville, CABAL ISLAND, Temple of The Serpent

Saga Three: Tubular—Book 10

Too Much Tubular!

Copyright © 2023 by BRAVE BOOKS
All Rights Reserved

Book Illustrations © 2023 by Ali Elzeiny
Map Illustration © 2021 by Ali Elzeiny

Published by BRAVE BOOKS
www.BRAVEbooks.com

ISBN: 978-1-955550-53-6 (paperback)

First edition published in the USA in 2023 by BRAVE BOOKS

Printed in Canada

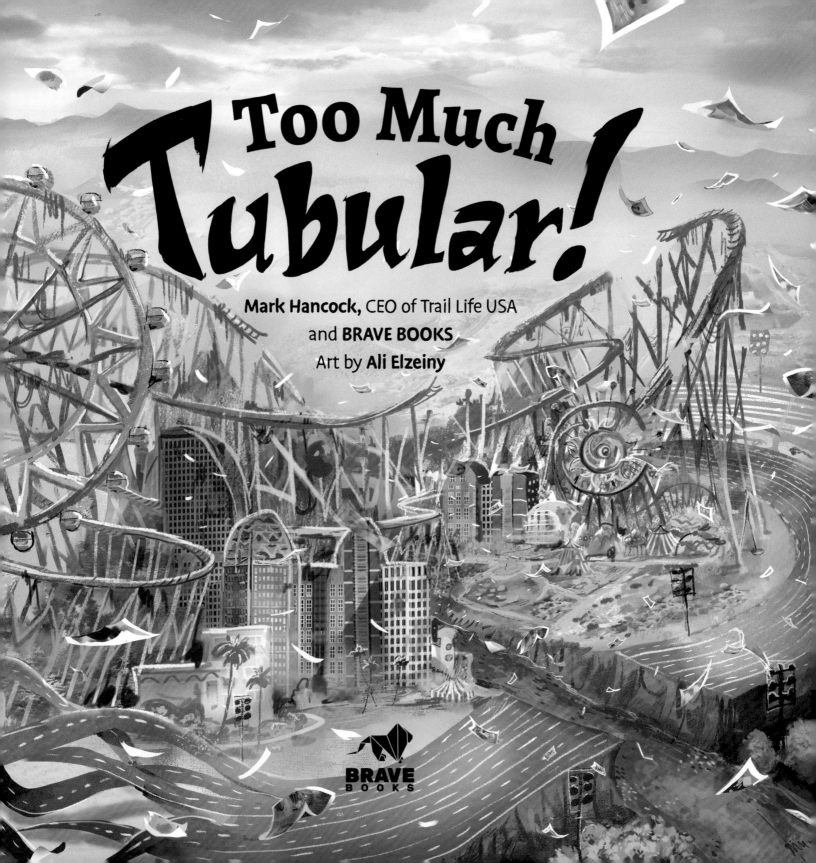

Too Much Tubular!

Mark Hancock, CEO of Trail Life USA
and **BRAVE BOOKS**
Art by **Ali Elzeiny**

BRAVE BOOKS

Photos blew across an empty courtyard as Team BRAVE stared at the broken rides and garbage littering the streets. They knew animals had become more and more obsessed with Tubular, Freedom Island's messaging system. But nowhere was as bad as Furenzy Park.

Almost overnight, it had turned into a wasteland,
and Team BRAVE was here to investigate.

"More! More!" a dazed bull groaned as it charged at them, clutching a Tubular photo.

Team BRAVE jumped out of the bull's path, just as he raced toward them.

"More! More!" a horde of animals yelled.

Frantically, Team BRAVE dashed into a gift shop and barricaded the door.

Valor the Tiger couldn't believe his eyes. "Did Tubular really cause all this?" he asked as he caught his breath.

"No, a Tubular obsession caused this," a mysterious voice said from the darkness.

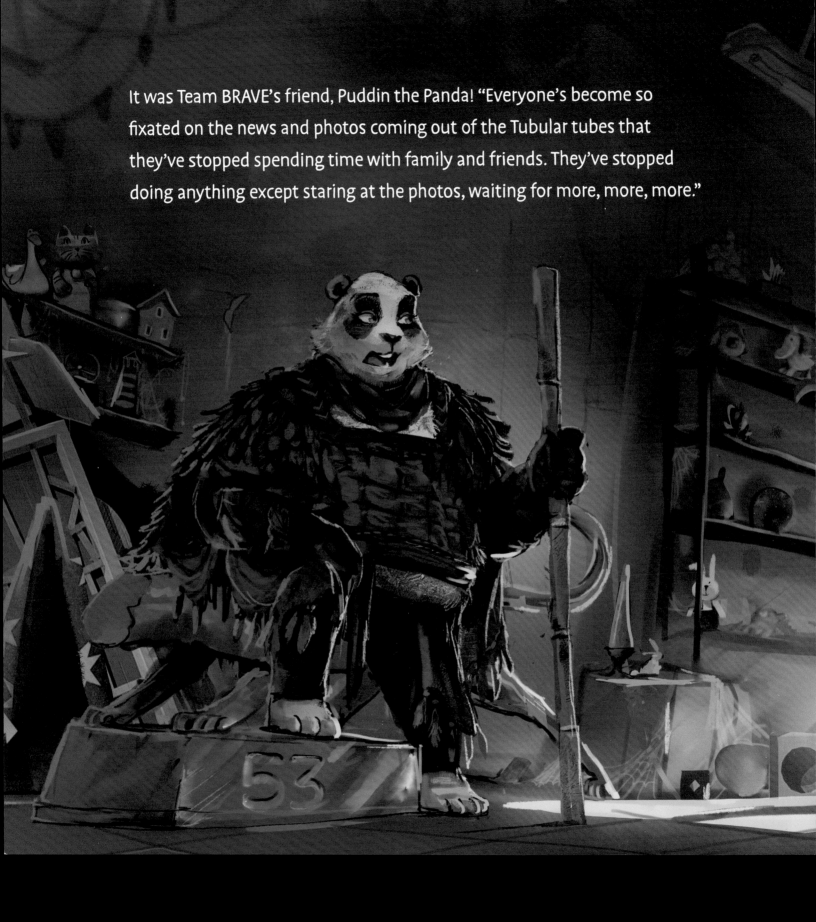

It was Team BRAVE's friend, Puddin the Panda! "Everyone's become so fixated on the news and photos coming out of the Tubular tubes that they've stopped spending time with family and friends. They've stopped doing anything except staring at the photos, waiting for more, more, more."

"That's horrible! We have to destroy Tubular," Valor exclaimed.

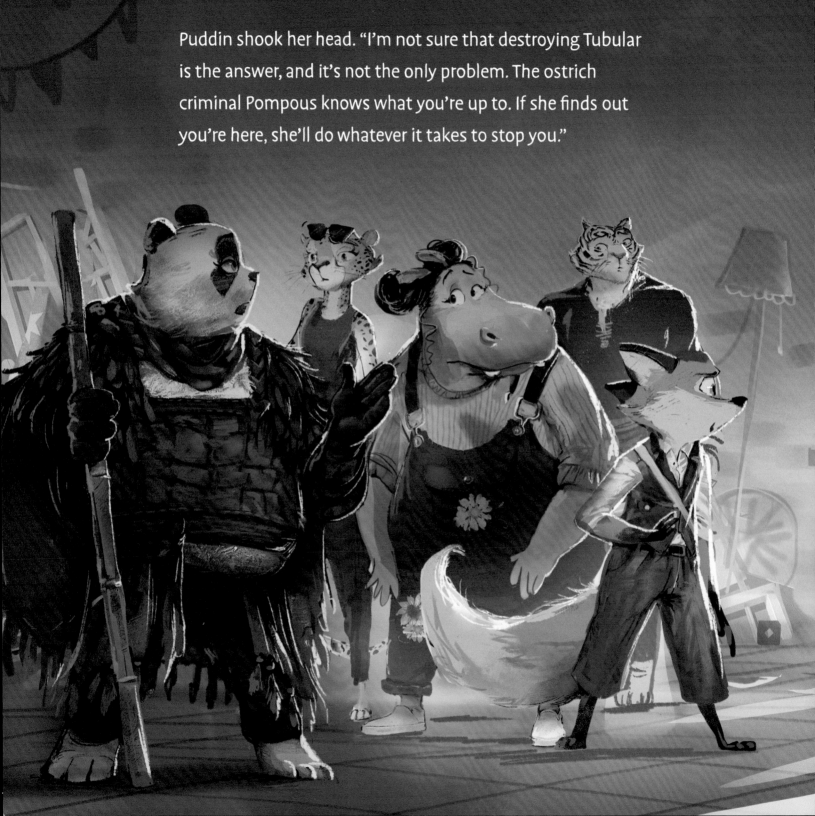

Puddin shook her head. "I'm not sure that destroying Tubular is the answer, and it's not the only problem. The ostrich criminal Pompous knows what you're up to. If she finds out you're here, she'll do whatever it takes to stop you."

Suddenly, a photo of Pompous shot out of a nearby tube.
Bongo gulped as he bent down to pick it up.

"Dudes, Puddin is right," Bongo said. "I think we've got a problem."

The doors burst open as animals clutching Tubular photos poured into the gift shop.

"Run! I'll hold them off!" Puddin yelled. "Go, Team BRAVE! Don't get distracted by the photos. Don't... hey, is that a bamboo recipe?" Puddin asked as a photo was shoved in her face.

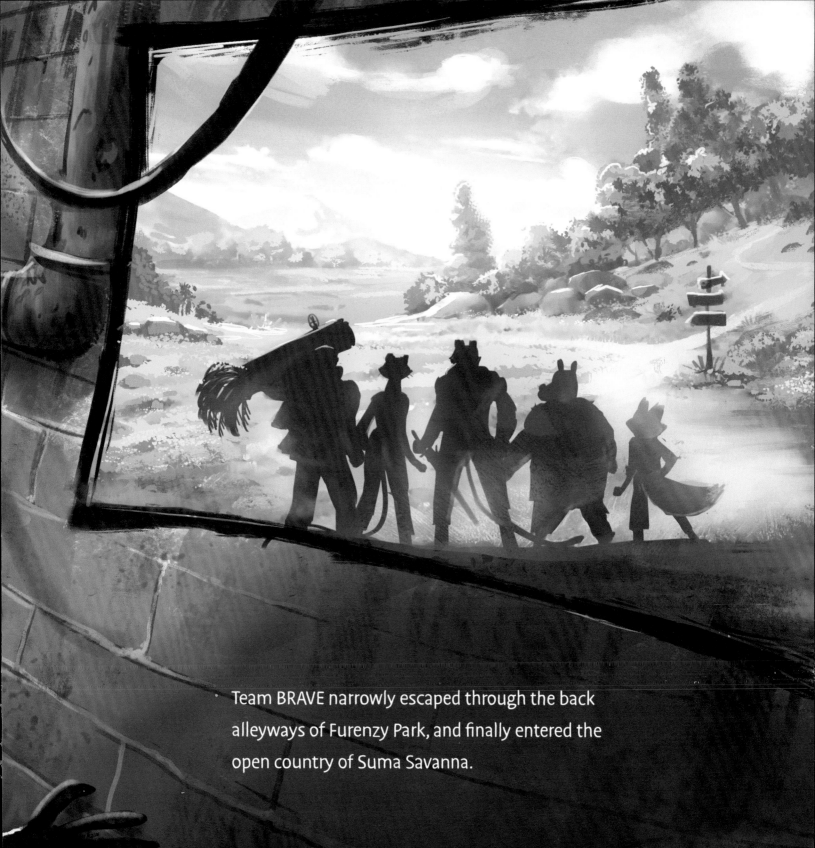

Team BRAVE narrowly escaped through the back alleyways of Furenzy Park, and finally entered the open country of Suma Savanna.

"Hello. Do you need some help?" asked a little hawk.

Bongo pointed toward Furenzy Park. "We have to destroy the Tubular tubes, or else our eyes will get all swirly, and we won't be able to bend our arms or legs!"

The hawk nodded. "Maybe my parents can help. My name's Fletcher. Want to come to our campsite for some s'mores?"

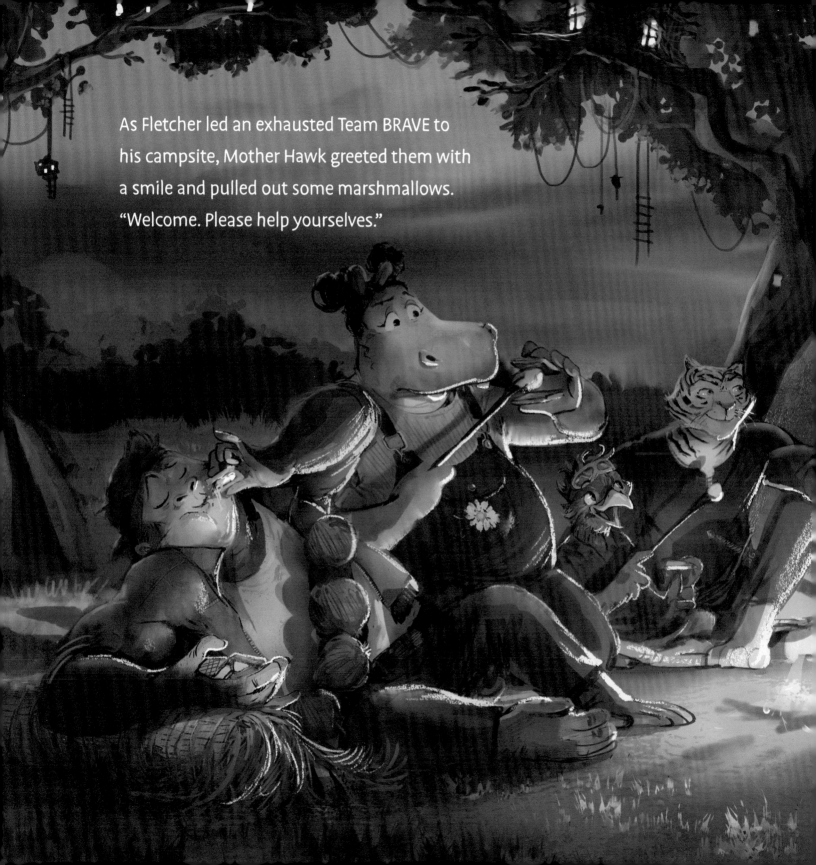

As Fletcher led an exhausted Team BRAVE to his campsite, Mother Hawk greeted them with a smile and pulled out some marshmallows. "Welcome. Please help yourselves."

Valor looked around. "Thanks … but why aren't you
guys obsessed with Tubular like everyone else?"

Father Hawk smiled. "We sometimes use Tubular, but we also enjoy spending time with family in the great outdoors. Maybe Tubular isn't the problem, but how one uses it."

"Yeah!" Fletcher took a big, messy bite. "I'd eat s'mores all the time if I could! But Mom says, only in maaaaw-der-ay-shuuun."

"Moderation! That's it!" Valor exclaimed. "I know how to fix this."

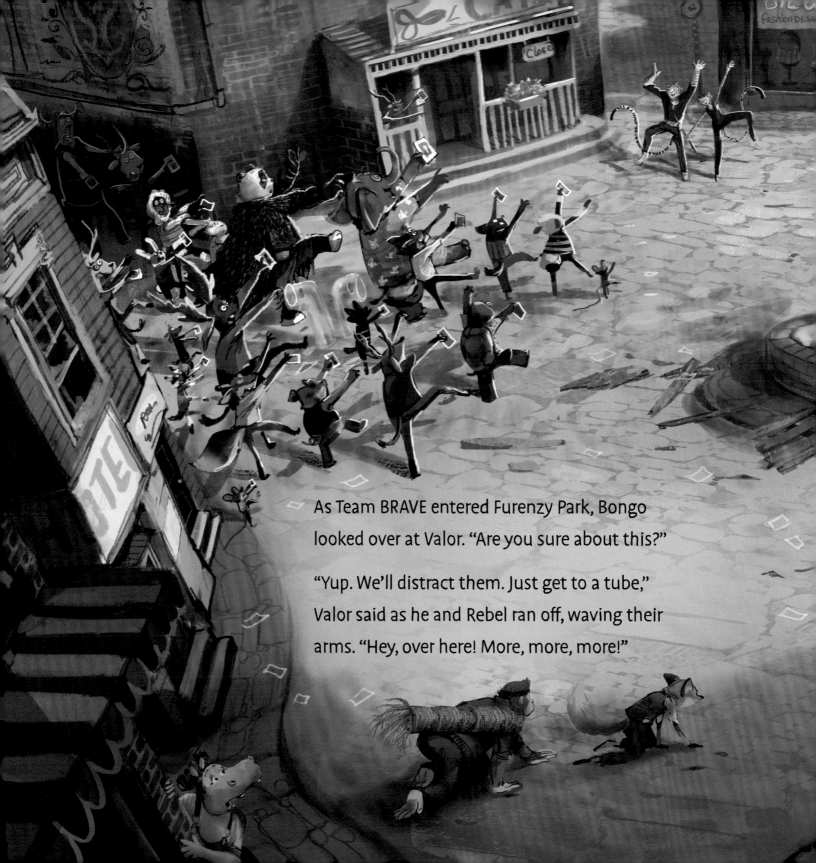

As Team BRAVE entered Furenzy Park, Bongo looked over at Valor. "Are you sure about this?"

"Yup. We'll distract them. Just get to a tube," Valor said as he and Rebel ran off, waving their arms. "Hey, over here! More, more, more!"

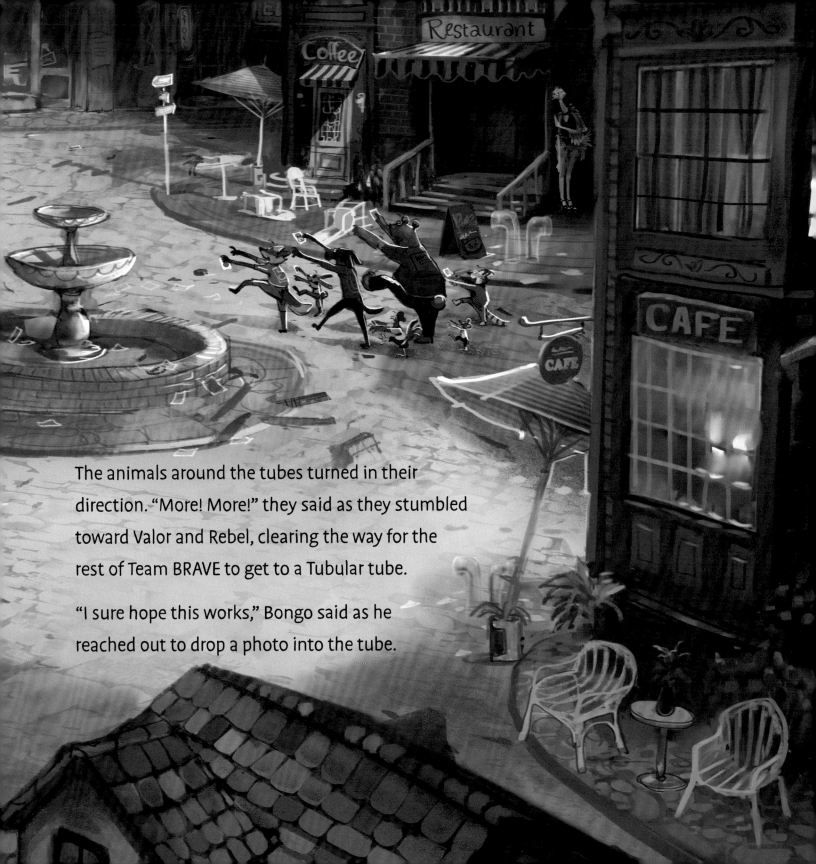

The animals around the tubes turned in their direction. "More! More!" they said as they stumbled toward Valor and Rebel, clearing the way for the rest of Team BRAVE to get to a Tubular tube.

"I sure hope this works," Bongo said as he reached out to drop a photo into the tube.

Puddin the Panda, still completely obsessed along with all of the other animals, pulled a new message from a tube.

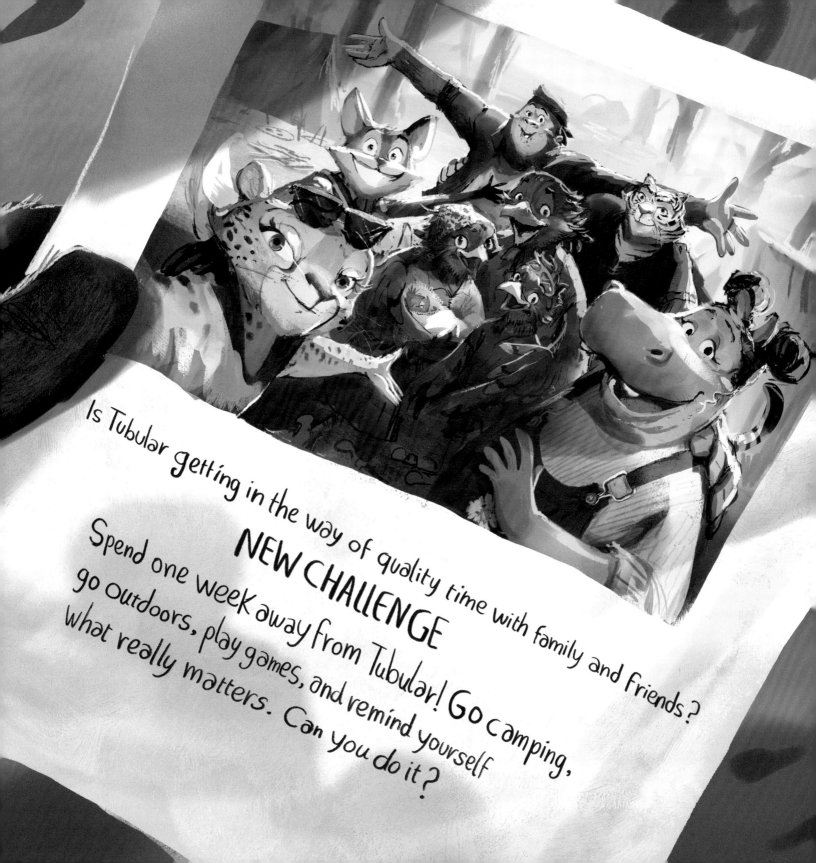

Is Tubular getting in the way of quality time with family and friends?

NEW CHALLENGE

Spend one week away from Tubular! Go camping, go outdoors, play games, and remind yourself what really matters. Can you do it?

As animals across Freedom Island received the challenge, they all began dropping their cameras and photos and walked away from the Tubular tubes.

One by one, they began to choose quality time with their families and friends rather than obsessing over Tubular.

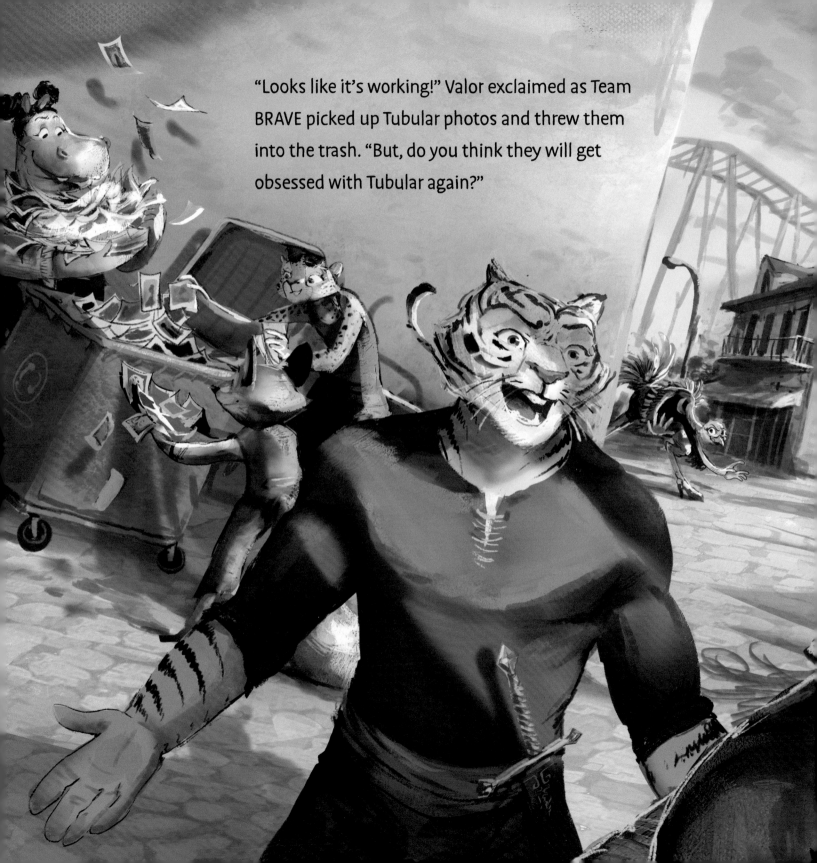

"Looks like it's working!" Valor exclaimed as Team BRAVE picked up Tubular photos and threw them into the trash. "But, do you think they will get obsessed with Tubular again?"

Bongo grinned. "I can't tell the future, bro, but I know we helped them see there's more to life than looking at pictures in front of a tube all day. We're made to spend time together, care for each other, and most importantly, share our desserts."

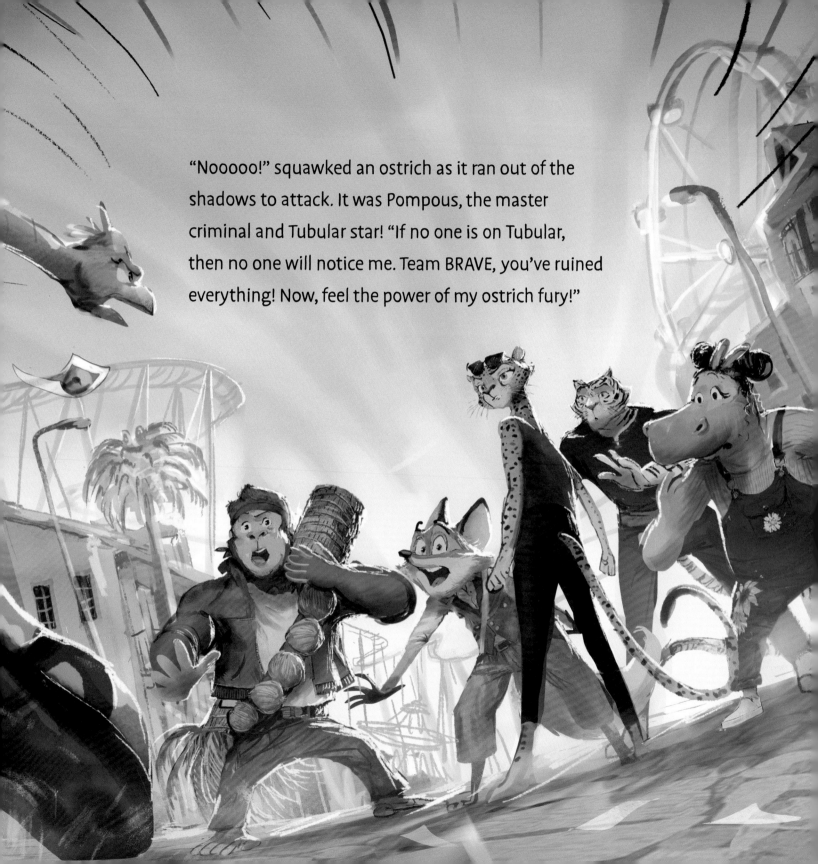

"Nooooo!" squawked an ostrich as it ran out of the shadows to attack. It was Pompous, the master criminal and Tubular star! "If no one is on Tubular, then no one will notice me. Team BRAVE, you've ruined everything! Now, feel the power of my ostrich fury!"

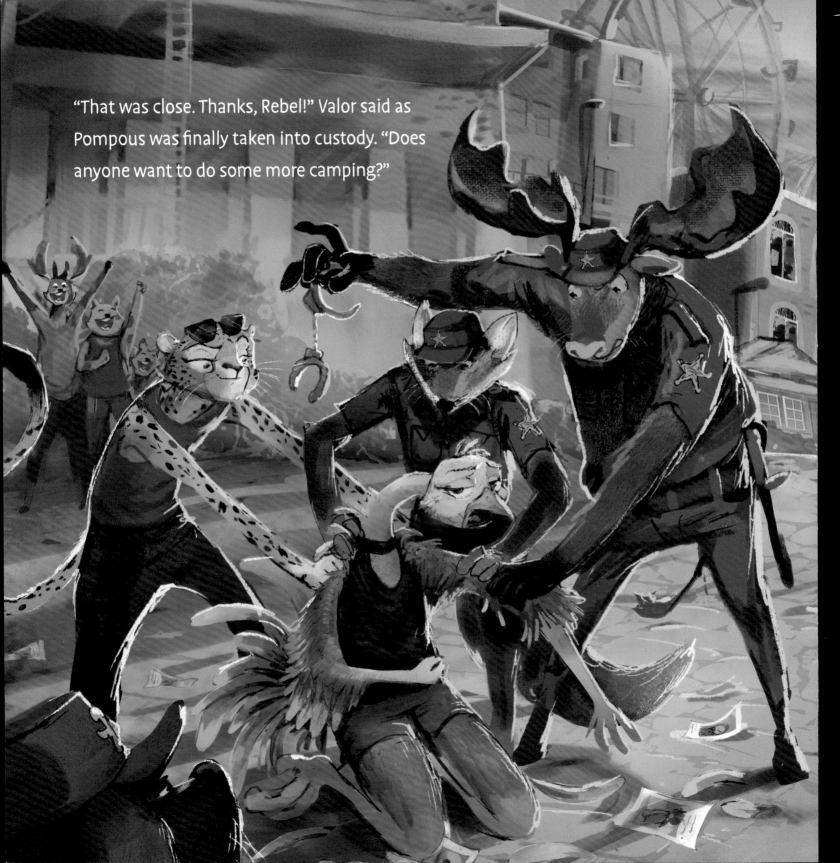

"That was close. Thanks, Rebel!" Valor said as Pompous was finally taken into custody. "Does anyone want to do some more camping?"

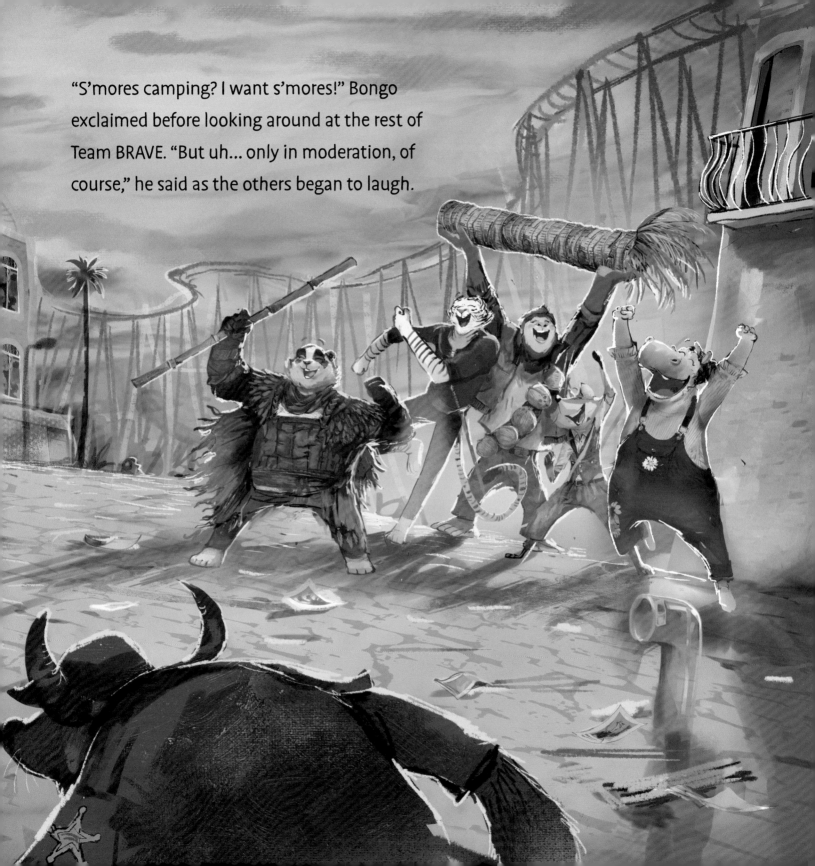

"S'mores camping? I want s'mores!" Bongo exclaimed before looking around at the rest of Team BRAVE. "But uh... only in moderation, of course," he said as the others began to laugh.

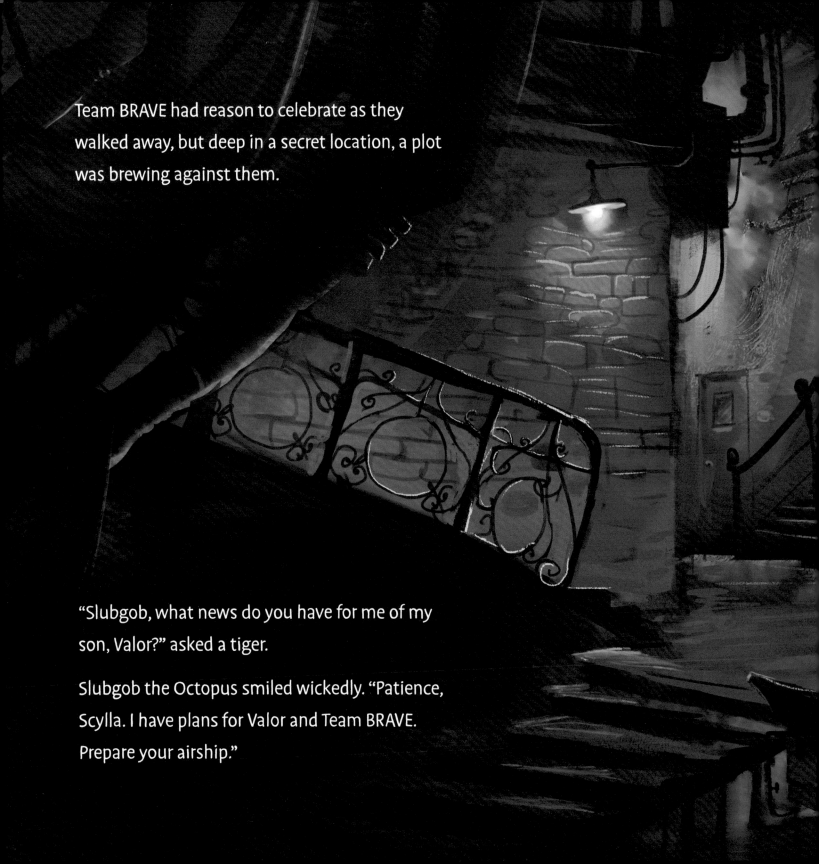

Team BRAVE had reason to celebrate as they walked away, but deep in a secret location, a plot was brewing against them.

"Slubgob, what news do you have for me of my son, Valor?" asked a tiger.

Slubgob the Octopus smiled wickedly. "Patience, Scylla. I have plans for Valor and Team BRAVE. Prepare your airship."

FURENZY PARK PRESS

Issue 10 • The Fastest Coverage of Furenzy Park

POMPOUS THE OSTRICH HAS BEEN FOUND AND ARRESTED

HELP WANTED: PARK CLEAN UP

In the wake of animals across Freedom Island pulling themselves away from Tubular, pictures continue to be littered around many major cities. For all those in and around the Furenzy Park area, we would like to ask for volunteers in helping clean up. Free Furenzy Park tickets will be given to those who participate! All help is welcome and appreciated.

TRAIL LIFE TRAILMEN LEAD TO NATURE

With the release of the new Tubular challenge, created by Team BRAVE, animals begin to spend more time outdoors and with family. To help guide them are the Trail Life Trailmen: Tracker, Fletcher, and Bramble. We at Furenzy Park thank them for helping us see nature clearly.

From Left to Right: Tracker, Fletcher, Bramble

BRAVE CADETS,

The animals of Freedom Island have learned how to balance their time well instead of being obsessed with Tubular. But that doesn't mean they won't become obsessed again. Complete the three missions below to help show the animals the importance of moderation:

- Update your map with the Slubgob and Scylla stickers included.

- Help Team BRAVE in the BRAVE Challenge, and celebrate your victory with an epic reward.

- Can you find Fletcher 5 times in the story?

Freedom Island is counting on you! Are you ready to be BRAVE?

5 NEAT LITTLE NATURE FACTS

1. Tigers have both striped fur and striped skin.

2. Pineapples can take two years to grow.

3. Most frogs can jump up to 20 times their height.

4. Acacia trees can warn each other of danger.

5. Carrots can also be red, white yellow, and purple.

CAN MONKEYS REALLY FLY?

According to a tourist from Rushington, they can! "Look, I'm not saying they had wings in which to fly with." Explained Tommy Toucan, "However, they were all on a large ship with a giant balloon attached to it, so technically they were flying." Eyewitness reports state that the airship was heading for Rushington, which also happens to be where Team BRAVE was last seen. Perhaps they can get some answers.

INTRODUCING...

TRAIL LIFE USA

Trail Life USA is a Christ-centered mentoring and discipleship journey that speaks to a boy's heart. Established on timeless biblical values and set in the context of outdoor adventure, boys from K-12 engage in a troop setting. Led by male mentors, they are challenged to grow in character, understand their purpose, serve their community, and develop practical leadership skills to carry out the mission for which they were created. Trail Life USA has joined with BRAVE Books in writing *Too Much Tubular!*, a book that teaches the importance of moderation and spending time with family.

TRAIL LIFE USA SUGGESTS:

"At Trail Life, we value how we spend our time and what we spend our time on. This book will help you and your family understand how we should balance our time and how we need to practice moderation."

INTRODUCTION

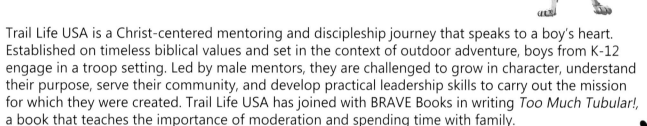

Animals at Furenzy Park have become obsessed with Tubular! Your mission is to encourage the Tubular-obsessed animals to use Tubular in moderation and make time for family and friends.

If your team wins both games, you have won the challenge and helped the Tubular-obsessed animals.

Before starting Game #1, choose a prize for winning. For example ...

- Going camping with the family
- Making s'mores
- Having a family game night
- Whatever gets your kiddos excited!

GAME #1 - WALK IN THE PARK

LESSON

It's important that we spend time with family and friends.

OBJECTIVE

When Team BRAVE meets Fletcher and his family, they realize that spending time with family will help the Tubular-obsessed animals. BRAVE Cadets, spend time with your family by playing this game.

MATERIALS

A timer.

INSTRUCTIONS

1. The parents represent the Tubular-obsessed animals at Furenzy Park, and the cadets represent Team BRAVE.

2. Play this game in a big open space and set up boundaries in the room.

3. Start a 2-minute timer. The parents must close their eyes and try to turn the cadets into Tubular-obsessed animals by touching them. The cadets can freely move around the room.

4. **Secret Step:** *Parents, make funny animal noises or say, "more, more" to try to make them laugh.*

5. If a parent touches a cadet, he or she becomes a Tubular-obsessed animal. The cadet must then close their eyes and try to turn the remaining cadets into Tubular-obsessed animals, too.

6. The game ends when the timer goes off or if all of the cadets have been turned.

TIME

Set a 2-minute timer to start the game.

SCORING

If at least one cadet is left standing when the timer goes off, the cadets win the game.

ONE CHILD MODIFICATION

Have one parent play with the cadet, and the other parent play the Tubular-obsessed animal.

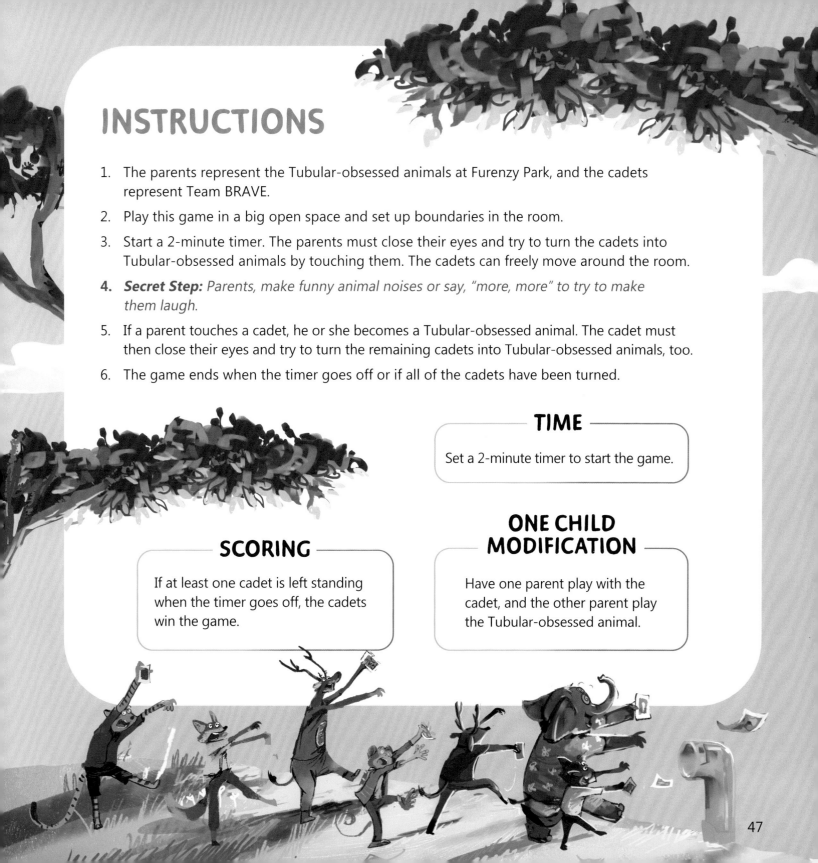

TALK ABOUT IT

1. In the game, you had to hide from the Tubular-obsessed animals. Could you imagine playing this game all by yourself? Do you have a game that you like to play with your siblings or parents?

2. What kind of things do families do together? Why is that important? How are your friends different from your family?

TRAIL LIFE USA SUGGESTS:

"God gave us families so we could enjoy fellowship together, help each other, and love each other. In addition, we learn how to care for and treat others because of the time we spend with our family."

3. In the story, Father Hawk told Team BRAVE that he would rather spend more time with his family than be obsessed with Tubular. Give examples of fun things that you do with your family.

4. What would be the Tubular tube (thing) in your life that distracts you from spending time with family?

5. How can you deepen your relationships with your family members?

 "Do nothing from selfish ambition or conceit, but in humility count others more significant than yourselves. Let each of you look not only to his own interests, but also to the interests of others."

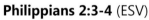

Philippians 2:3-4 (ESV)

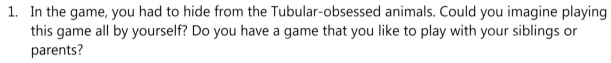
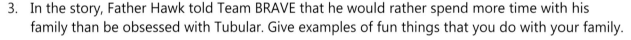

GAME #2 – FOOD MENU OVERLOAD

LESSON

Too much of anything is bad.

OBJECTIVE

The animals of Freedom Island are becoming obsessed with Tubular photos. BRAVE Cadets, help Team BRAVE show the animals what it looks like to have too much by planning your next meal.

INSTRUCTIONS

1. Have the cadets sit in a circle.

2. Choose one cadet in the circle to start the game. They must say, "I am going to eat …" and then say their one of their favorite food. For example, "I am going to eat ice cream."

3. The cadet on their left must repeat what the first cadet said and then add on one of their favorite food. For example, "I am going to eat ice cream and brownies."

4. Repeat this process with every cadet by going in a circle and adding to the food menu.

5. The game ends when a cadet messes up the food menu or when they reach the score to win the game.

ONE CHILD MODIFICATION

Have the parents play with the cadet.

SCORING

If the cadets are younger, they must add 5 food items to the menu to win the game.

If the cadets are older, they must add 8 food items to the menu to win the game.

TALK ABOUT IT

1. In the game, you had to add a bunch of your favorite foods to the menu. Could you eat all of that food at once? What do you think moderation is? Do you think it would be wise to eat all of the food at once?

2. Do you have a toy or game that you play with a lot? Why can it be hard to put it away? Is it wrong to play with that toy? When does it become too much of a distraction?

TRAIL LIFE USA SUGGESTS:

"How we spend our time shows us what we love and treasure. If we love our family, we will want to spend time with them. If we love a video game, we will spend time playing it. It's not wrong to enjoy the things we have, but when we become obsessed with them, we spend more time with them than we should."

"Do not lay up for yourselves treasures on earth, where moth and rust destroy and where thieves break in and steal, but lay up for yourselves treasures in heaven, where neither moth nor rust destroys and where thieves do not break in and steal. For where your treasure is, there your heart will be also."

Matthew 6:19-21 (ESV)

3. Why did the animals spend most of their time by the Tubular tubes? What were they sacrificing by spending their time looking at the photos?

4. How much time do you spend on an electronic device or playing with a toy? How much time do you spend with your family?

TRAIL LIFE USA SUGGESTS:

"It's important to take a step back and look at where we spend our time. Here's your challenge: Try to keep track of how much time you spend playing with an electronic device or toy and how much time you spend with your family for a week. At the end of the week, look at where your time has been spent to see if you need to change any habits."

BRAVE CHALLENGE COMPLETE!

FINAL THOUGHTS FROM TRAIL LIFE USA

God calls us to be stewards of our time, and in Ephesians 5:15-16 (ESV), He says, "Look carefully then how you walk, not as unwise but as wise, making the best use of the time, because the days are evil. Therefore do not be foolish, but understand what the will of the Lord is." It can be hard to overcome obsession sometimes, but God can give us the strength and wisdom we need when we spend time in His Word, prayer, and fellowship with other believers.

Learn more about Trail Life USA by visiting

traillifeusa.com